Rod and Staff Books

(Milestone Ministries)
800-761-0234 or 541-466-3231
www.RodandStaffBooks.com

FARMING with FATHER

FARMING with FATHER

By Rosene L. Burkholder

Artist: Martha J. Kuhns

ROD AND STAFF PUBLISHERS, INC.
P.O. Box 3, Highway 172
Crockett, Kentucky 41413
Telephone (606) 522-4348

Printed in U.S.A.

ISBN 0-7399-0399-X

Catalog no. 2234

6   7   8   9   —   17   16   15   14   13   12   11   10   09

TABLE OF CONTENTS

Welcome to Winding Glen Farm 10

1. Surprise! 13

2. Call the Doctor 23

3. Chore Time 35

4. Doctor's Helper 52

5. Under the Willow 59

6. The Parting 72

7. Breakdowns! 84

8. "Let's Trade" 94

9. Prayers Answered 101

10. Partners 114

FARMING with FATHER

My name is Henry Cunningham.
    I live at Winding Glen
With Father, Mother, Baby Tim,
    And little sister Gwen.

This farm is where my father lived
    From birth till wedding day;
Then he and Mother made a home
    A couple miles away.

But he came over here to work
    Until a recent year
When Father's parents moved away;
    Now we are living here.

I like to live at Winding Glen;
    I'm glad we're here to stay.
Now I can help around the farm
    Most any time of day.

CHAPTER 1

Surprise!

The day is dawning warm and bright
When Mother taps my door.
She wakens me with cheery voice:
"It's nearly time to chore."

I stretch a little, yawn a bit,
And scramble out of bed.
The rooster cock-a-doodle-doos
To skies of gold and red.

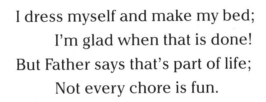

I dress myself and make my bed;
    I'm glad when that is done!
But Father says that's part of life;
    Not every chore is fun.

I hurry out to feed the dog,
    But where could Lassie be?
I like to make her jump for bones
    And shake a paw with me.

"Here, Lassie, Lassie, Lassie girl."
  Ah, here she comes, I see.
She dashes up across the yard
  And stops in front of me.

"Now, Lassie, sit!" She promptly sits,
  Extends to me a paw;
Then—*woof!*—she leaps to snatch the bone
  And settles down to gnaw.

16

It's time to feed the woolly sheep;
　　They're bleating near the gate.
I think if they could talk they'd say,
　　"The farmer boy is late."

　　　　I quickly fill the water trough
　　　　　　And haul a load of hay.
　　　　They crowd around me while I work;
　　　　　　What hungry sheep are they.

My other chores are in the barn;
    It's milking time, you see.
I swing the barn door open wide;
    The cows look up at me.

"Good morning, Son," my father says;
    A twinkle lights his eyes.
"If you will look in Flossie's pen,
    You'll see a nice surprise."

18

I hurry back to find the cow,
And guess what else I see!
A pair of calves on wobbly legs,
As cute as they can be.

I stroke each black and silky head,
Each little velvet nose;
And when I'm least expecting it,
They lurch and tramp my toes!

19

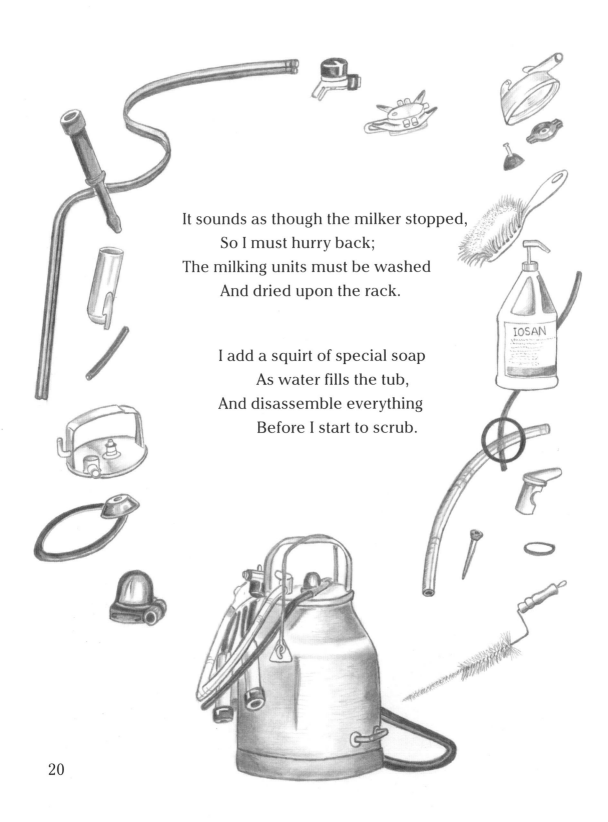

It sounds as though the milker stopped,
  So I must hurry back;
The milking units must be washed
  And dried upon the rack.

I add a squirt of special soap
  As water fills the tub,
And disassemble everything
  Before I start to scrub.

I brush each piece and rinse it well.
I need to get them clean,
For there could be a smelly mess
If milk remains, unseen.

The scrubbing done, I pull the plugs
    To start a favorite chore.
As water swishes round my boots,
    I quickly sweep the floor.

    The water swooshes down the drain;
        My early chores are done.
    When Father says, "It's breakfast time,"
        I grab my cap and run.

CHAPTER 2

Call the Doctor

The smell of bacon beckons me
Before I reach the door,
But first I wash my face and hands
And use the comb some more.

It seems I hear a happy squeal
From Baby Timmy's crib.
"Get Timmy, Henry," Mother says,
"And find for him a bib."

I peek around the bedroom door
And hoarsely whisper, "Boo!"
Then Timmy turns and, seeing me,
Begins to smile and coo.

I scoop him up and carry him
To his appointed chair.
He tries to eat his froggy bib
As he is waiting there.

When everyone has gathered round,
    We sing our morning prayer.
We thank the Lord for daily food
    And tender loving care.

"Oh, yummy, scrambled eggs again,
    On top of buttered toast.
It seems you know the way to cook
    To please a fellow most."

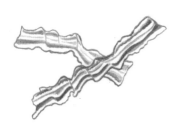

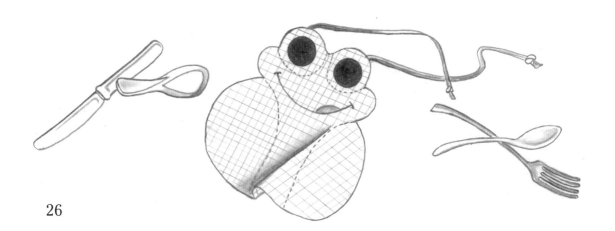

"Well, thank you, Henry," Mother says.
   "I always try to plan
A menu that will help you grow
   To be a healthy man."

When everyone has had enough
   And every plate is clean,
I take the Bibles off the shelf,
   The hymnals covered green.

27

"Let's turn to Daniel," Father says,
  "And chapter 3 today;
It's Henry's turn to pick a song
  And Mother's turn to pray."

When everyone has found the place,
  We read the verses there.
We join to sing "The God We Serve;"
  Then Mother leads in prayer.

Today we read about a king
  Who made an image grand.
And then a call to worship it
  Went out across the land.

But there were three who loved the Lord,
Whose hearts were brave and true;
In spite of fiery furnace threats,
They knew what they would do.

When music played, the others knelt,
But these refused to bow.
They trusted God at other times,
And they would trust Him now.

Another chance was offered them
To serve the image here,
But they declared their trust in God
Without a trace of fear.

Enraged, the king commanded men
To make the furnace *hot!*
And those who threw the Hebrews in
Were slain upon the spot.

The flames destroyed the captives' ropes
 But spared the foot and hand;
And Someone came from God above
 To join this little band.

The king, astonished, rose in haste
 And called them out again.
He ordered everyone respect
 The God who saved these men.

The God they served is here with us!
 His care is still the same
For all His children everywhere,
 Who love and fear His Name.

31

It's time to wash the dishes now
And put the books away.
My father also has some chores
For me to do today.

The dishes washed, I hurry out
To check my favorite cow.
The calves are stepping here and there,
But Flossie's resting now.

It seems that Flossie's getting sick;
   Just see her droopy eyes!
I gently nudge her silky rump;
   She tries in vain to rise.

I hurry off to Father's shop,
   And Father calls the vet.
He says that he will treat our cow,
   But he cannot come yet.

33

Then Father looks at me and says,
   "I really ought to plow.
So clean the barn, and stay around
   To help him treat the cow."

        Then down the lane the tractor roars
           To chisel-plow the sod.
        My father wants to plant some beans
           And prays for rain from God.

CHAPTER 3

Chore Time

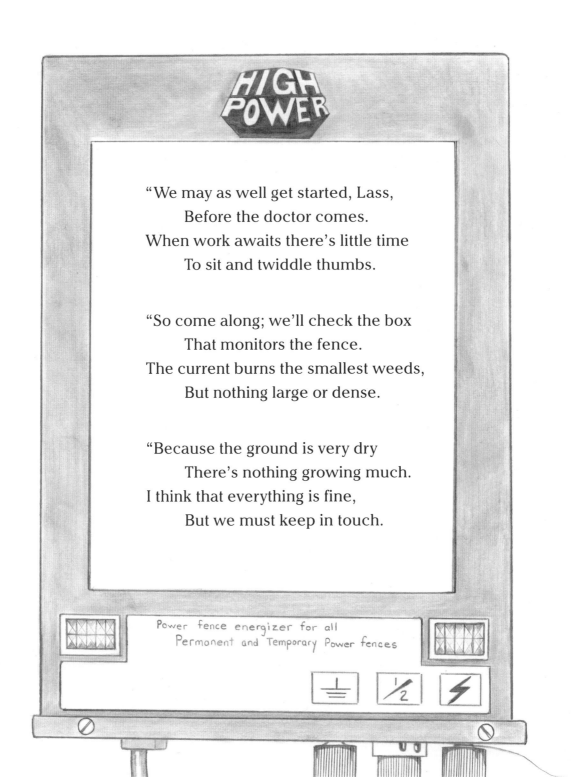

"We may as well get started, Lass,
Before the doctor comes.
When work awaits there's little time
To sit and twiddle thumbs.

"So come along; we'll check the box
That monitors the fence.
The current burns the smallest weeds,
But nothing large or dense.

"Because the ground is very dry
There's nothing growing much.
I think that everything is fine,
But we must keep in touch.

Power fence energizer for all
Permanent and Temporary Power fences

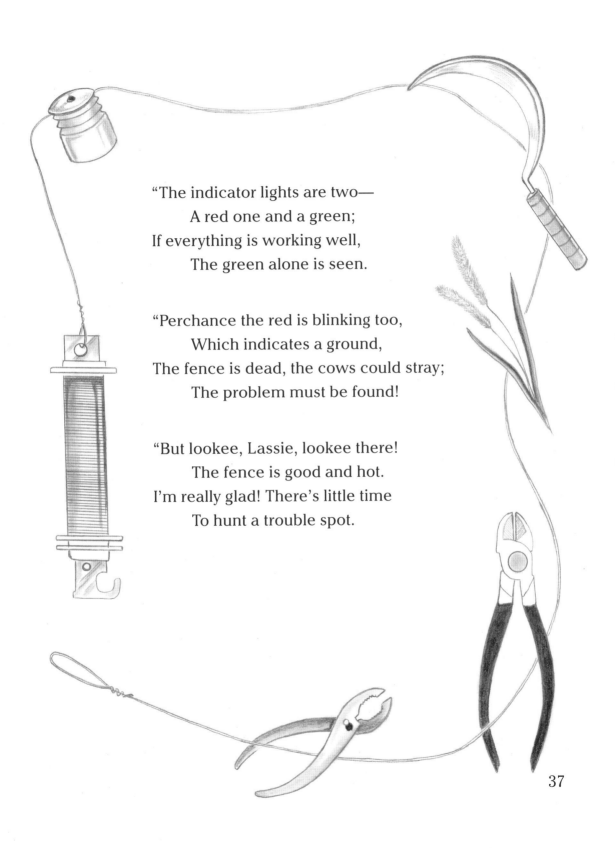

"The indicator lights are two—
    A red one and a green;
If everything is working well,
    The green alone is seen.

"Perchance the red is blinking too,
    Which indicates a ground,
The fence is dead, the cows could stray;
    The problem must be found!

"But lookee, Lassie, lookee there!
    The fence is good and hot.
I'm really glad! There's little time
    To hunt a trouble spot.

"Since yesterday was Sunday, Lass,
    We didn't load manure.
So now the gutters must be cleaned;
    Of that we can be sure!"

        I flip the switch, the chain responds,
           Conveyers start to go.
        They move the litter up the chute
           Till—*plop!*—it falls below.

The spreader's hitched and waiting there
　　To catch another load,
Which nowadays my father spreads
　　On land across the road.

　　Since everything is working well,
　　　I'll let the cleaner run.
　　I'm going now to clean the barn
　　　Before the job is done.

The scraper hangs, with fork and broom,
    Along the western wall;
I need to scrape an aisle or two,
    And then I'll sweep them all.

    A center aisle divides the barn,
        With room on either side
    To milk a herd of forty cows;
        The stalls are nice and wide.

The smaller aisles at either end
    Connect the feeding lanes,
And all along the southern wall
    Are many windowpanes.

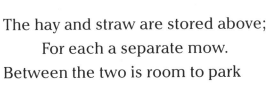

The hay and straw are stored above;
    For each a separate mow.
Between the two is room to park
    The baler, disc, and plow.

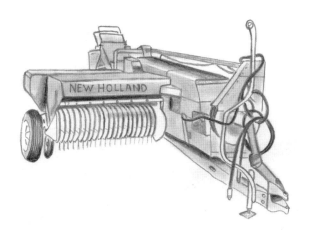

The stable looks deserted now
    Compared to milking time.
A cat named Queenie suns herself
    Across a bag of lime.

That litter pile is getting high;
    I'll pull the spreader front.
I climb the tractor, turn the key;
    But all I hear is *grunt*.

Well, what can be the matter now?
   It simply will not start!
I guess I'll need to get the fork
   And tear the pile apart.

So here I go inside again!
   I'm glad the fork's in place.
Remember, tines must downward point
   And never toward the face.

43

Outside, I reach across the sides
  And fork the smelly stuff.
It's not a very pleasant job;
  I think I've done enough.

I flip the little switch again
  To let the cleaner run,
And level off the growing pile
  Until the job is done.

JOHN DEERE

44

The stable cleaned, I climb the steps
For several bales of straw;
I send them diving through the hole
And watch them while they fall.

The first one hits the floor—*kerplunk!*
The second bounces high;
The third one topples end for end
And clean escapes my eye.

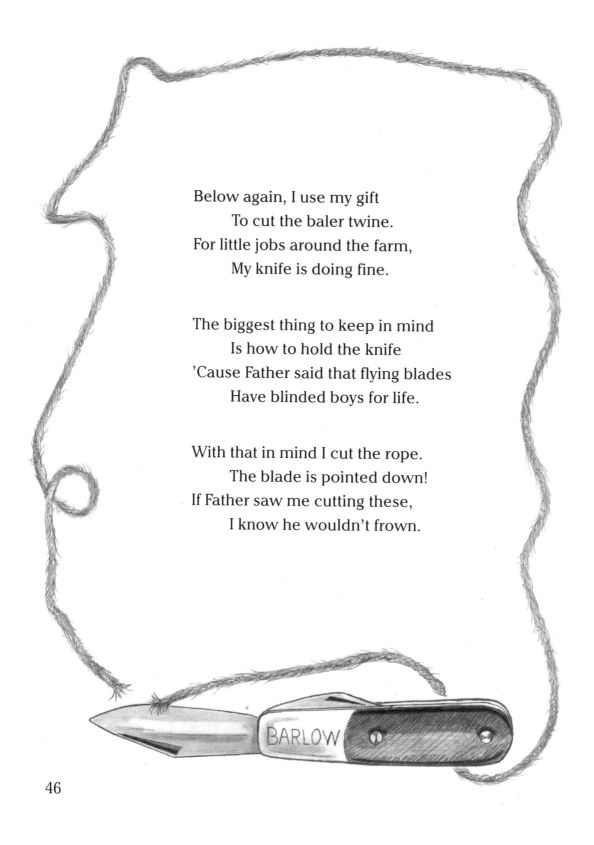

Below again, I use my gift
    To cut the baler twine.
For little jobs around the farm,
    My knife is doing fine.

The biggest thing to keep in mind
    Is how to hold the knife
'Cause Father said that flying blades
    Have blinded boys for life.

With that in mind I cut the rope.
    The blade is pointed down!
If Father saw me cutting these,
    I know he wouldn't frown.

BARLOW

And now it's time to use the fork
    To spread the chunks of straw;
The gutter cleaner works the best
    With bedding under all.

I hang the fork and take the broom
    To sweep away the crumbs.
It looks as though my chores will end
    Before the doctor comes.

47

'Tis not the day to spread the lime,
    So now the chores are done.
I think I'll bring my scooter here
    And take a little run.

The stalls are splendid parking lots
    Along the center street.
The feeding lanes are country roads;
    The cats are folks I meet.

But soon I hear a scratching sound
As Lassie paws the door;
Her basket holds a little note:
"I need some eggs. Get four."

With Lassie trotting close to me,
　　We reach the chicken house;
While I am finding Mother's eggs,
　　The collie hunts a mouse.

　"Come, Lassie girl," I say to her,
　　　"This job is yours to do.
　You take the eggs to Mother now;
　　　I think she waits for you."

The collie likes this little game.
    She gently pads away
And takes the eggs that Mother needs,
    For this is baking day.

        She sets the basket down with care
            And dashes back to me;
        She wants to play another game,
            But now a car I see.

51

CHAPTER 4

Doctor's Helper

It's Doctor Johnson here at last!
I quickly lead the way
To Flossie, who is lying down
And doesn't eat her hay.

"I hope that Flossie soon gets well."
My voice betrays my fear.
The doctor eyes our Holstein cow
And gently feels her ear.

"A treatment should be all she needs;
    She's not as sick as some.
But if she doesn't soon get up,
    You call and I will come."

The doctor feels her silky neck
    And slides a needle in.
Poor Flossie shakes her weary head
    And tries to look at him.

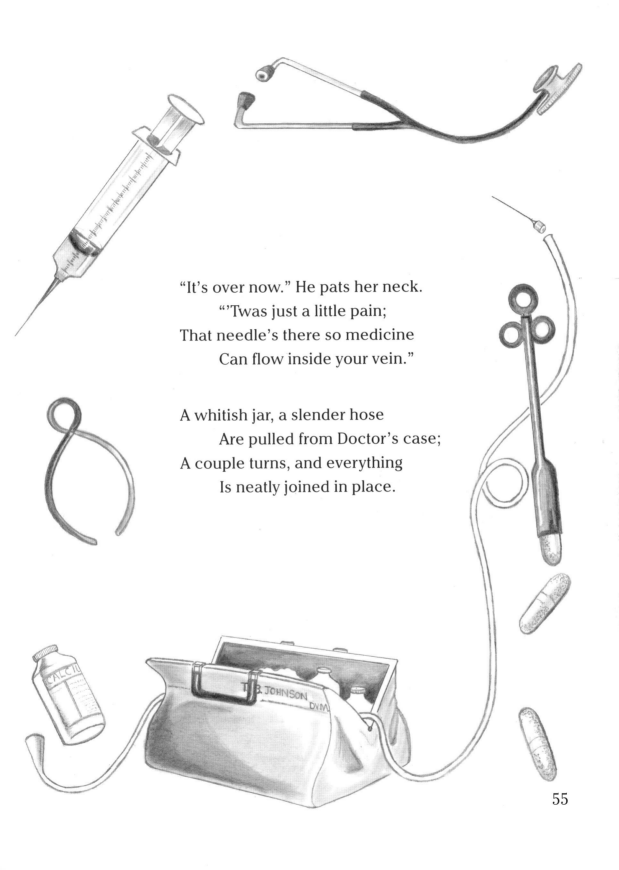

"It's over now." He pats her neck.
"'Twas just a little pain;
That needle's there so medicine
Can flow inside your vein."

A whitish jar, a slender hose
Are pulled from Doctor's case;
A couple turns, and everything
Is neatly joined in place.

Then Doctor turns to me and says,
"Here's just the job for you!
Please hold this jar of calcium;
I've something else to do."

I take the jar and lift it up
To fill the slender hose.
The liquid moves at turtles' pace;
Into the vein it flows!

I keep the jar above my head.
    My arm begins to ache;
But well I know if I would sag
    The longer this will take!

A fuzzy, buzzing bumblebee
    Explores the calving pen.
The swallow Doctor scared away
    Returns to nest again.

At length the jar of medicine
    Is emptied through the hose.
I tell him, "Thank you very much,"
    And soon the doctor goes.

He's out of sight when all at once
    My stomach starts to growl.
It must be nearly dinnertime;
    I'll go to Mother now.

CHAPTER 5

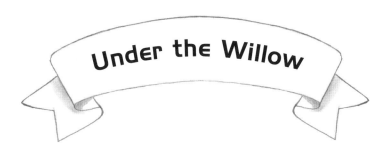

Under the Willow

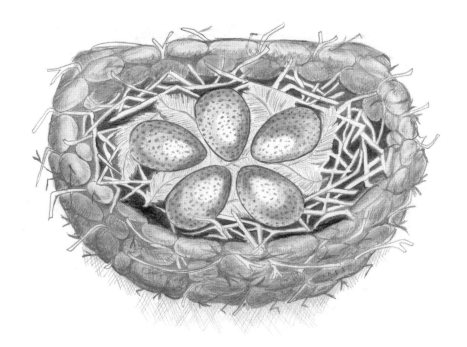

My sister's wrapping whoopie pies,
　　While Mother slices meat;
I see a bag of carrot sticks
　　And other things to eat.

"We planned a picnic," Mother says,
　　"Beneath the willow tree.
When Father sees us waiting there,
　　He'll join us too, you see."

"Oh, goody! Goody! Picnic lunch!"
　　We laugh and clap with glee.
I quickly get the yellow jug
　　To fill with meadow tea.

　　The picnic lunch is ready soon;
　　　　My wagon's waiting too.
　　My sister gathers plates and cups,
　　　　The tablecloth that's blue.

"That's everything," says Mother now,
And shuts the basket—*snap!*
"Now load the wagon while I bring
The baby from his nap."

I load the picnic basket first,
And next the yellow jug;
In front is room for Baby Tim,
A place that's safe and snug.

But now my sister starts to beg,
"I wanna ride with Tim!"
So I remove the picnic jug
And let her sit with him.

I start to pull the wagonload,
And Mother takes the drink.
The sun's so bright for Baby Tim
It makes him sneeze and blink.

63

Our journey takes us past the barn
　　And by the calving pen.
I see that Flossie can't get up
　　But chews her cud again.

We trudge along the dusty lane,
　　Through short and crunchy grass;
The grazing cows look up to watch
　　Our bumping wagon pass.

At last we reach our chosen spot—
    The willow's welcome shade.
The winding brook flows gently by
    Inviting me to wade.

    The water cools my dusty feet;
        It tickles sister's toes.
    She starts to kick excitedly,
        And droplets splash her nose.

Along the lane as Father comes
    He lifts a cloud of dust.
The ground is very, very dry!
    I hope it rains. It *must!*

The beans that Father wants to plant,
    The corn that's in the field—
They all need lots of gentle rain
    To make them grow and yield.

He lets the tractor idle now
    A distance from the tree.
Our baby's glad to see him come,
    And so, of course, are we.

We bow our heads as Father prays,
 And then begin to eat.
The willow's shade and Mother's lunch
 Are such a pleasant treat.

A cow appears and pausing there
 Observes our tasty meal;
She briefly eyes the tractor too
 And sniffs a dusty wheel.

67

She ambles on to join the cows,
    Beneath the maple tree;
But while I view those dusty wheels,
    A question troubles me.

"Oh, Father, is there any use
    To ask the Lord for rain?
He hasn't sent a single drop;
    It seems we pray in vain."

But Father slowly shakes his head.
   "We never pray in vain,
For God has promised He will hear
   Requests in Jesus' Name.

"The Lord delights to answer prayer
   Today and every day.
When times are good, when times are bad,
   It always helps to pray.

"It may not be the way we think
That God will answer prayer,
But He who sees the sparrow fall
Will keep us in His care.

"So we will pray, 'Thy will be done,'
And plan to calmly wait.
At proper time we'll gather in
The harvest, small or great."

Returning Father's smile, I nod
    And lean against the tree.
My father trusts in God above,
    And that's enough for me.

Then very soon our meal is done,
    Since Father needs to plow.
He gives me chores that I should do.
    "And don't forget the cow!"

71

CHAPTER 6

The Parting

When I have pulled the wagon home,
I'm free to start the chores.
I climb the hill behind the barn
And swing the wooden doors.

As sunlight floods the second floor,
The shadows flee away;
A startled pigeon seeks a hole
That's high above the hay.

73

I start to sweep the parking bay
    That's strewn with chaff and straw;
"'Tis good precaution," Father says,
    "In case a spark should fall."

It's such a dusty job—*ker-choo!*
    Looks like there won't be much;
I load the straw—*ker-choo, ker-choo!*–
    And wheel it toward a hutch.

These roly-poly hutches stand
    Like bubbles in a row,
Awaiting Flossie's heifer calves;
    A place to live and grow.

I dump the load inside a hutch
    And go to sweep some more.
I work until a golden mat
    Is spread across each floor.

75

It's time again to check the cow.
    Hurrah! She's looking great!
She's able now to join the herd;
    I quickly swing the gate.

I thread my way between the calves
    To turn the cow around.
"Get moving, Flossie. Time to go!"
    But Flossie stands her ground.

I thump a stick against her leg
    To start her walking through;
She slowly moves, but soon I hear
    A soft and mellow *moo*.

Then just before she leaves the pen,
    She turns and circles back!
The second time we near the door,
    I give her rump a whack.

She hurries through the open door;
I slam and bar the gate.
When Flossie circles back again,
She's just a bit too late.

She thrusts her head across the bars
And sadly bellows *moo-o-o*.
Her heifers, sensing something wrong,
Bewail the parting too.

"Keep moving, Floss. It bothers me
To hear you bawling so;
But Father said to chase you out,
So, Floss, you have to go!"

She plods on slow, reluctant feet,
But doesn't venture far
Beyond the painted barnyard fence,
To where the others are.

79

It surely was a miracle
    When back in Israel's day
Those mothers left their little calves
    And took the ark away.

I close the fence and hurry back
    To finish sweeping straw,
But every now and then I hear
    Her brokenhearted bawl.

I climb the steps to get some bales
    To further line the "nest";
I want to make a fluffy bed
    Where Flossie's calves can rest.

I pause to wipe my sweaty face;
    I'm getting tired and hot.
A whoopie pie and meadow tea
    Would really hit the spot!

On second thought, I'd better work;
  It doesn't pay to poke.
When I have finished spreading straw,
  I'll rest beneath the oak.

The second hutch is nearly done
  When Sister brings a treat!
The thought of rest and food and drink
  Gives wings to weary feet.

She helps to spread the final bale;
    At last the job is done.
We put away the cart and broom,
    And toward the tree we run.

Why, sure enough she brought me tea
    And yummy whoopie pies.
When every bite has disappeared,
    I close my sleepy eyes.

CHAPTER 7

Breakdowns!

"Oh, Henry, Henry! Get awake!
 The ram has gotten out!
Oh, now he's jumping back again.
 I guess he heard me shout."

I rub my eyes and look around;
 But thanks to little Gwen,
The ram has joined the other sheep
 Inside the fence again.

By now my nap's deserted me;
    There's nothing left to do—
Why, here is Father coming back;
    It's only half past two!

"I hoped to finish," Father says,
    "But I must fix the plow.
I hit a rock and broke a tooth.
    I'll go to Hartman's now.

"Yes, Henry, you may go along
    If all your work is done.
Tell Mother that we're taking Gwen,
    And please be sure to run!"

When I return, we hop aboard,
    And Father drives away.
I like to go along to town
    At any time of day.

I watch the fields and homes go by—
　　But who is this ahead?
We reach the car beside the road,
　　And, lo, it's Brother Fred!

"I'm glad you stopped," he says to us.
　　"I prayed that someone would.
The car got hot, but these old hands
　　Could scarcely lift the hood."

Then Father says he's glad to help;
    He'll see what he can do.
A check reveals a broken hose
    With water leaking through.

    "I think the hose is long enough
        To stretch a little bit,
    But I should have a pocket knife
        To make a better fit."

89

A pocket knife? I reach for mine
    So he can trim the end.
I'm glad that he can use my knife
    To help our stranded friend.

He cuts away the tattered part
    And clamps the hose in place.
We're glad to see the shorter hose
    Still fits across the space.

"The radiator's fairly hot;
    So while the engine cools,
We'll get the water," Father says,
    "A couple bucketfuls."

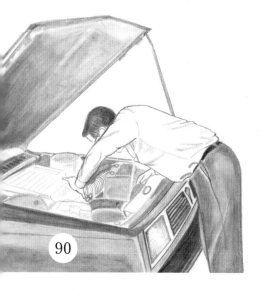

We drive to Grandpa Cunningham's,
    A mile or two ahead,
To see if Grandma has some pails
    To fill for Brother Fred.

She gives an empty pail to Gwen,
    Another one to me;
She knows we like to use the pump
    That's near the apple tree.

We pump the handle up and down;
    The water gurgles up.
Then *splash*, it fills our little pails
    And brims the drinking cup.

I wish that we could stay a while,
　　But we must not delay.
We wave good-bye to Grandma now
　　As Father drives away.

　　The radiator's cool enough;
　　　　It doesn't hiss or spray;
　　When he removes the little cap,
　　　　We're out of danger's way.

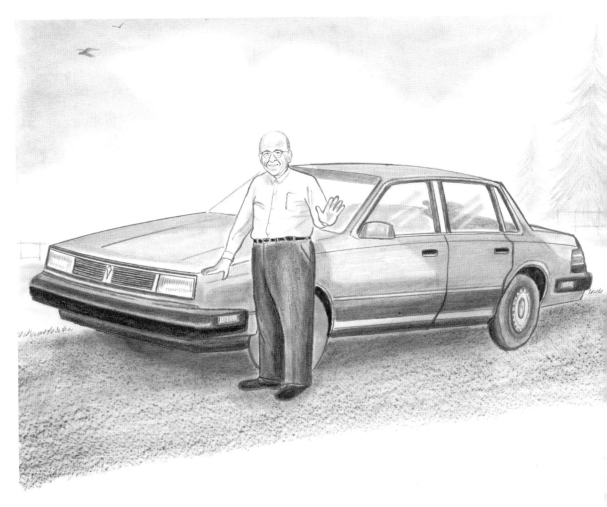

We quench the radiator's thirst
  And drop the heavy hood.
"I'm very grateful!" Fred exclaims.
  "The Lord reward you good."

When Brother Fred is homeward bound,
  We also drive away.
I think that all of us are glad
  We helped our friend today.

CHAPTER 8

"Let's Trade"

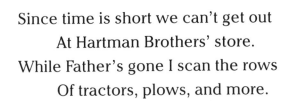

Since time is short we can't get out
At Hartman Brothers' store.
While Father's gone I scan the rows
Of tractors, plows, and more.

"A Uni-loader! See it, Gwen?
It's sitting over there.
The paint is hardly scratched at all;
The seat has little wear."

She glances there, but merely nods
Before she looks away
To watch the folks at Tastee Freeze
Who bought a treat today.

Oh, goody, here is Father now.
"Just see that loader there?
The boys say that kind is the best
And all the rest are fair.

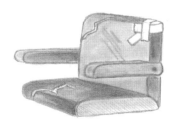

"The seat on ours is getting bad;
  The paint is dull and thin.
Let's get the one that's over there,
  And trade our old one in."

"Let's talk a little," Father says
  While smoothly shifting gears.
"We bought our loader secondhand
  And used it several years.

"The tires are good, the engine runs,
  The job is getting done;
So is there any reason yet
  To buy another one?"

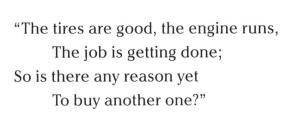

"Well, no, there isn't," I reply.
    "It doesn't look the best;
But since it does the job at hand,
    I'll let the matter rest."

"Contentment, Son, is what we need
    When friends begin to talk;
Contentment mixed with trust in God
    Will cheer our daily walk."

98

We're driving through the country now,
    Where men are cutting wheat.
I think I see our neighbor Joe
    On yonder combine seat.

    A semi waits to haul the grain,
        Another drives away;
    And over there . . . "Oh, Father, look!
        The sky is turning gray!"

"Why, so it is! And see that tree!
Your Grandpa used to say
A maple tree with silver leaves
Means rain is on the way."

We scan the sky with hopeful eyes
As down the road we go;
The grayish clouds stretch on and on,
And gentle breezes blow.

CHAPTER 9

Prayers Answered

Arriving home, there would be time
To help to fix the plow.
But Father says I ought to chore;
A storm is brewing now.

I run behind the milking barn
And down the dusty lane.
I need to get the herd of cows
Before it starts to rain.

My ear is tuned to thunderclaps,
    Which say a storm is near;
But Flossie's loud and mournful wail
    Is all that I can hear.

If we could milk at normal time,
    The cows would start for home;
But most of them are resting now.
    A few prefer to roam.

103

Approaching Kate, I wave my arms.
"Get up! It's time to go!
Get started, Betsy. Take the lead!
Get moving, Pat and Jo!

"Now, Buttercup"—I slap her rump—
"You ought to get in gear!
We're going to have a thunderstorm,
So let's get out of here!"

I wave and shout to rouse the cows
    Beneath the maple tree;
But they would rather chew their cuds,
    And that is plain to see!

I try to shoo them toward the barn.
    I work with all my might!
They take a little step or two
    And stop to grab a bite.

If only Lass would come around—
 "Get moving, Muffin. Shoo!"
I can't go back and leave them here—
 "Keep going, Pat and Sue!"

  It seems to be a hopeless case;
   They won't obey today.
  But what did Father say at noon?
   "It always helps to pray"!

"Dear God, I have a problem here;
   The cows have stopped again.
If 'tis Thy will, please help me now.
   In Jesus' Name. Amen."

And then a plan begins to form:
   Since Betsy leads them all,
If she would—Listen, what was that?
   It's Father's morning call!

They perk their ears at Father's voice;
    He bids them "Come" and "See."
(He uses this to bring them home
    Instead of Lass and me.)

    The cows respond and head for home
        As nicely as can be;
    And soon we're thirty, forty feet
        Beyond the maple tree.

Then all at once the quiet air
   Explodes with deaf'ning sound.
As lightning cracks and thunder booms,
   A tingle fills the ground.

I cringe beneath the dreadful noise—
   Now what is that I smell?
And then I see that lightning struck
   The tree they liked so well.

The maple has a jagged scar
That's longer yet than I,
Where lightning tore a limb away.
I fear the tree will die!

The cows? Why, look! They're running home!
They're really scared, I know!
Just see the way they hold their tails.
Just look at Betsy go.

A flash of lightning startles me—
The barn's the place to be!
Before the thunder starts to roll,
I turn around and flee!

I reach the barn in record time,
And bursting through the door
I sprawl across the bags of lime
As rain begins to pour.

I notice then, with great relief,
That all the cows are here.
A few are panting even yet;
Their eyes are wide with fear.

"Oh, thank You, God, for helping me!
If cows had been instead
Beneath the tree when lightning struck,
They likely would be dead!"

I leave my perch to tie some cows—
Amanda, Sue, and Jane;
But now and then I pause to sniff
The pleasant smell of rain!

"Oh, here you are," says Father now.
"I'm glad that you are back.
I didn't know the storm was close
Before that dreadful crack."

And then I pour my little tale
In Father's list'ning ear.
"Well, thank the Lord," he soon replies,
"That all of you are here!"

CHAPTER 10

Partners

With all the cows securely tied,
    We pause to watch the rain.
It drums against the metal roof
    And streaks the windowpane.

"Let's thank the Lord for sending rain!"
    My father scans the sky.
"It seems we farm as partners, Son:
    The Lord and you and I.

115

"I spread manure and plow the field
    Before I sow the seed,
But only God can send the sun
    That growing plants will need.

    "A man may choose to irrigate,
        But still he needs the rain
    So his intended water source
        Will not be caused to drain.

116

"The part that's left for you, my son,
   You handled well today;
I know that I can count on you
   When I must be away."

   "Oh, Father, I will do my best.
      Your partner I will be!"
Exchanging smiles, we turn to go;
    It's time to milk, you see.